The Adventures of
Amber
WALK IN THE WOODS

The Adventures of Amber: Walk in the Woods
Copyright © 2021 by Isabell Hayden. All rights reserved.

Illustrations by Bekir Rıza Şahin

Published by Mindstir Media, LLC
45 Lafayette Rd | Suite 181| North Hampton, NH 03862 | USA
1.800.767.0531 | www.mindstirmedia.com

Printed in the United States of America
ISBN-13: 978-1-7370915-8-5

The Adventures of
Amber
WALK IN THE WOODS

Isabell Hayden

illustrated by Bekir Rıza Şahin

MINDSTIR MEDIA

Her name is Amber.

Amber is an adventurous girl who loves *NATURE*.
She has a cute sidekick, her pup, Daisy.

During summer, Amber visits her grandparents' cottage in the mountains. Taking an afternoon walk in the woods with her grandma and her pup is Amber's favorite thing to do.

"Grandma, are you ready for a fun adventure in the woods this afternoon?" Amber asks joyfully.

"Yes, of course, **LET'S GO!**"
Grandma happily replies.

Taking walks in the woods is so much fun!
There are **magnificent** evergreen
trees in the woods.

Looking up at the trees,
Amber says in wonderment,
"The trees are so

Beautiful birds are sitting on tree branches. Amber gets up close
to have a better look at the birds.
"Tweet, tweet, chirp, chirp!"
The birds are having a good time singing happy tunes.

As Amber, Daisy, and Grandma wander in the woods, they pick up leaves, twigs, and seeds that have fallen to the ground. "Grandma, we can make an art project with these!" Amber says excitedly.

"Yes, of course! What a great idea, Amber," Grandma agrees.

After a long walk, they sit under a BIG leafy tree to rest their legs and enjoy the beautiful trees, flowers, and insects.

There are brown mushrooms and green moss
under the trees.

The moss feels like a soft blanket.

Sunlight shines between the tree
branches, and tiny flying insects dance
under the sunbeams.

"Wow!" Amber says, as she and Daisy look at a big ant climbing on a leaf.

"Grandma, there is a GIANT ant!" Amber exclaims.

Amber and Grandma lean back in the grass and look to the sky. Amber blurts out, "Look how fluffy those clouds are!"

"Yes, the clouds are very fluffy," Grandma agrees and asks, "What do they look like to you?"

"They look like cotton candy." Pointing toward one, Amber giggles and says, "This one looks like a sheep and that one looks just like Daisy!"

"Quack, quack, quack!" By the lake, baby ducklings have fun splashing in the water and playing with the mommy ducks. Daisy barks. She wants to jump into the lake to play too.

Amber, Grandma, and Daisy walk along a creek, enjoying the sounds of the stream as it softly pitter-patters along. A gentle breeze kisses their faces.

In a field, Amber, Grandma, and Daisy look at colorful wildflowers and bright-red, itsy-bitsy wild strawberries.

They are not the only visitors in the field. Butterflies, hummingbirds, and bees play hide-and-seek in the flowers.

The sun starts to set.

The frogs in the pond begin to croak loudly,

It is a frog singing contest.

Croak, Croak, Croak!

It is time to head back.

"Look, Grandma! Daisy flowers!" Amber exclaims.
"Daisies for Daisy!"
Amber's walk with Grandma and Daisy was magical,
and finding daisy flowers for Daisy at the end of their walk
was a special treat.

Many animals call mountains their home.
Here are a few of Amber's favorite animals.

Yellow Warblers—Yellow warblers are beautiful yellow birds. They are small, but they know how to sing beautiful tunes. They hop between tree branches and twigs to find caterpillars and other insects to eat. Both mommy and daddy yellow warblers are loving parents. They take turns feeding and taking care of their baby yellow warblers.

Blue Jays—Blue jays are beautiful and smart. They are omnivorous, which means they eat both plants and other animals. Their favorite foods are fruit, nuts, insects, and even mice. Blue jays are very protective parents. They fearlessly guard their nests against any hawks, raccoons, cats, squirrels, or other animals that may hurt their baby blue jays.

Ruby-Throated Hummingbirds—Ruby-throated hummingbirds are tiny. They only grow to about three inches long. They drink nectar from flowers and sometimes eat small insects and spiders. These hummingbirds can fly backward and upside down. They can also hover in one place, like a helicopter. They have short legs, so they are not good at walking or hopping.

White-Tailed Deer— White-tailed deer are shy. They have good eyesight and hearing. They can run away quickly when they sense danger nearby. Mommy white-tailed deer are very loving and protective of their baby deer. When mommy deer go away looking for food, they put their baby white-tailed deer in a good hiding spot so predators cannot spot them easily. While waiting for their moms to return, baby deer lie flat on the ground with their necks stretched out flat to camouflage (blend in) with the forest floor.

North American Porcupines—North American porcupines are very good at protecting themselves because they have quills (sharp and pointy spines) that predators do not want to get too close to. They like to spend their time alone. They are friendlier during the winter when they share homes and feed with other porcupines. North American porcupines are herbivores, which means they eat only plants, such as leaves and evergreen needles. Porcupines have long claws and are good climbers. They climb trees to find delicious leaves to eat.

Red Foxes— Red foxes like to be alone. They do not form packs like the wolves. Red foxes are good communicators. They know how to make many different sounds to communicate with other red foxes. They also make sounds to let their babies know when there is danger nearby. In addition to having good eyesight and a good sense of smell, red foxes also have a good memory, as they are very good at remembering where they have hidden or stored their food. Their favorite foods are rabbits, birds, and rodents.

BioKIDS. Accessed February 10, 2021. www.biokids.umich.edu/critters/
Washington NatureMapping Program. Accessed February 10, 2021. www.naturemappingfoundation.org/natmap/
The Chesapeake Bay Program. Accessed February 10, 2021. www.chesapeakebay.net/
NatureWorks. Accessed February 10, 2021. www.nhptv.org/natureworks/
Animal Diversity Web (ADW), Accessed February 10, 2021. www.animaldiversity.org/

Thank You for Reading

I hope you enjoyed this book. I had fun writing it.
A portion of the book proceeds will be donated to
St. Jude Children's Research Hospital.

Acknowledgments

For Grandma and Grandpa, my loving
grandparents, thank you for the fun times that we
spent together.

For Rachel, my creative writing teacher, I've
learned so much from you, and you've made
learning fun too! Thank you.

For Mom and Dad, thank you for all the love and
support. I love you

Isabell

About the Author

Isabell Hayden is a child author. She loves to draw, dance, read, and write. Isabell also enjoys building LEGOs with Dad, baking cupcakes with Grandma (while wearing matching aprons), solving challenging puzzles with Grandpa, playing beautiful tunes on the piano for her pup, Daisy, and, last but not least, reading a good book with Mom. Isabell hopes to write more books to share her love of nature and all things fun and creative.

www.isabellhayden.com

About the Illustrator

Bekir Rıza Şahin is from the beautiful city of Antalya, Turkey. His love and passion for art began at a young age. When he was in elementary school, he would draw pictures that he liked. In middle school, he drew a comic book about the adventures of pirates. The characters in the book were his classmates. His passion for art continued through high school and college. His beautiful illustrations have been featured in many local magazines and publications. In addition to drawing beautiful illustrations, he also produces quality graphic design professionally.

graphicatorus@gmail.com